Jasmine Kettles

a treasury of
bedtime stories
& rhymes

A catalogue record for this book is available from the British Library

Published by Ladybird Books Ltd
27 Wrights Lane London W8 5TZ
A Penguin Company

© LADYBIRD BOOKS LTD MCMXCIX

Stories in this book were previously published by Ladybird Books Ltd
in the *Stories for Under Fives* series.

LADYBIRD and the device of a Ladybird are trademarks of Ladybird Books Ltd

a treasury of
bedtime stories
& rhymes

Ladybird

Contents

Farmyard Stories
by Joan Stimson
illustrated by Rebecca Archer

Bedtime
Stories

Contents

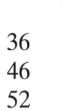

The runaway mouse

"I'm just popping out for some supper," said Mrs Mouse.

And a few minutes later she staggered back with a huge hunk of cheese.

"Ooooh!" squeaked five small voices. "Can we have some now, Mum?"

"No, you can't," said Mrs Mouse. "This cheese is for supper."

But the smallest mouse couldn't wait.

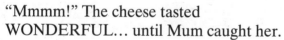

"Mmmm!" The cheese tasted
WONDERFUL… until Mum caught her.

"BED!" cried Mrs Mouse. "And no more
cheese for a week!"

The little mouse felt so sorry for herself that
she bolted right out of the family hole into the
big wide farmyard.

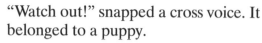

"Watch out!" snapped a cross voice. It belonged to a puppy.

"I'm running away," the little mouse told him. "Mum shouted. She said I couldn't have any more cheese."

"But did she stop you playing football?" asked the puppy.

The little mouse looked surprised and shook her head.

"Well, think yourself lucky. Mine did. And just because I was a bit rough. Would YOU like to be goalkeeper?"

The little mouse took one look at the tangle of puppies on the lawn and carried on running. She ran so fast that she almost fell into the duck pond.

"Going for a swim?" quacked a glum voice.

The little mouse shook her head.

"Nor me," said the duckling. "I'm not allowed in today. And just because I was a bit cheeky. But I could teach YOU how to dive."

The little mouse shivered as the other ducklings swam by. Then she carried on running.

"Not so fast!" hissed a black and white calf.

"I can't stop!" squeaked the little mouse.
"I'm running away. Because Mum shouted."

"I wish I could shout!" hissed the calf.
"I MOOED a bit too loudly last night. And
now I'm only allowed to *whisper*!"

"WOW! Was that noise ALL YOU?" cried
the little mouse. "You woke everyone up and
frightened us. Mum had to bring us a
midnight feast and tell us another…"

"WHOOSH!" Suddenly the little mouse felt so homesick that she ran all the way back to her hole. She dived straight into bed with her brothers and sisters and was just in time for a… STORY!

Cock a doodle help!

Cock a doodle do!
We don't know what to do.
Our rooster's lost his sense of time
And shouts at half-past two!

Cock a doodle pain!
…there he goes again.
Granny's packed her bags and gone,
She caught the early train!

Cock a doodle Dad!
My dad is hopping mad.
If Rooster went away as well,
I know that he'd be glad!

Cock a doodle Vet!
Please help us with our pet.
Check out his pulse and test his clock
(But don't make him upset!)

Cock a doodle hey!
He crowed at DAWN today.
He's back to normal, thank you, Vet,
Your skill has made our day!

21

Cat's cradle

Dad was taking Ben to choose a kitten.

The kittens had been born on a houseboat. And their owner wanted to find homes for them... before they jumped overboard!

Ben pointed to a handful of white fluff with a black patch.

"That one," he said. "And I'll call him Pirate."

Pirate liked living with Ben. But he didn't like his basket.

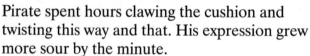

Pirate spent hours clawing the cushion and twisting this way and that. His expression grew more sour by the minute.

"Perhaps Pirate's cold," said Ben. He opened the airing cupboard door and lifted the kitten inside.

Pirate poked about among the clean washing. Then he arched his back and gave a loud sniff of disgust.

23

"Perhaps Pirate's missing his mum," said Dad.

So he got out Ben's old carrycot. Dad surrounded Pirate with baby blankets and gave him a big blue rabbit.

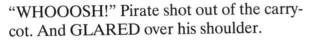

"WHOOOSH!" Pirate shot out of the carry-cot. And GLARED over his shoulder.

Pirate couldn't stand the sofa. He thought the beds were a dead loss.

And, although he snatched the odd catnap, Pirate never had a really good sleep.

Then one day Pirate went missing.

Ben and Dad searched the house from top to bottom. Next they tried the garden.

"Whatever's that noise?" said Dad. He looked across at the washing line.

"IT'S PIRATE!" cried Ben. "He's been asleep in the peg bag and he's PURRING!"

Dad watched Pirate swinging gently in the breeze.

"Of course," he said. "I should have known. Pirate is missing the feel of the water."

That evening Dad made a pint-sized hammock. He slung it between the beams in Ben's room.

"What do you think, Pirate?" asked Ben.

Pirate didn't claw or sniff or glare or disappear.

He just climbed into his hammock. And went to bed happily ever after!

27

Is Mr Marshall a Martian?

It was too hot to sleep. It was too hot even to read her new space book. So Lucy knelt down and gazed out of the window.

Next door Mrs Marshall was still gardening. At last she stretched and put away her rake. Lucy was just beginning to feel drowsy, when something else caught her eye.

It was a shadowy figure in the Marshalls' garden. And she was sure the figure was wearing a space helmet!

Lucy shot back into bed. Her book lay open on the pillow.

"IS THERE LIFE ON MARS?" it said.

Lucy slammed the book shut and pulled up the sheet.

For the next few evenings Lucy looked out at the Marshalls' garden… from behind her curtains.

But all she saw was Mrs Marshall weeding and Mr Marshall cutting the grass.

"I must have dreamt it," said Lucy.

But Lucy spoke too soon. There it was again… the same shadowy figure and the same space helmet!

Lucy fumbled under the bed for her telescope. But the figure had disappeared into the bushes. And all Lucy could see was a pair of boots… big silver boots which sparkled in the evening sunlight.

Lucy lay on her bed and thought what to do
next.

Before she could decide, there was a ring at
the door.

DING-A-LING-LING!

"I've come to borrow some cable."

It was Mr Marshall, talking to Dad. Lucy
dashed downstairs. She would tell them both
at once. After all, it was only fair to warn the
Marshalls.

Lucy burst into the living room.

"Whatever is it?" asked Dad.

But Lucy only gasped… because Mr Marshall was wearing boots… big silver boots which glinted against the dark carpet!

Lucy fled back upstairs.

"Is Mr Marshall a Martian?" she asked herself over and over again.

Then there were other, more confusing, questions.

"Why doesn't Mr Marshall wear his space helmet ALL the time? And where does he keep his spaceship?

"Oh no!" groaned Lucy suddenly. "His spaceship must be broken. And I bet it needs some NEW CABLE!"

Lucy fell into a troubled sleep before Dad could tuck her in. She woke late and anxious next morning.

DING-A-LING-LING! Dad went to answer the door.

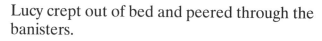

Lucy crept out of bed and peered through the banisters.

Mr Marshall looked pleased with himself. He handed Dad a jar with a homemade label.

"MARSHALL'S PRIZE HONEY," it said, and there was a picture of a huge bee.

"Good heavens!" cried Dad. "Don't you worry about getting stung?"

"Not with my special beekeeping helmet and boots," said Mr Marshall. "They work a treat… even if they do make me look like someone from outer space!"

All day long Lucy felt rather silly. That evening she tried to spot Mr Marshall's beehives from her window. The Marshalls looked up from their garden and waved.

When Dad came to tuck in Lucy, he was holding an invitation.

"Tom's having a fancy dress party," he said. "But we don't have anything for you to wear."

"Mr Marshall does," cried Lucy brightly. "I'll ask if I can borrow his beekeeping helmet and boots. And I'll go as a MARTIAN!"

35

Jake and the jumble panic

"Where's Wilfred?" shouted Jake at bedtime.

Wilfred was a battered bear with blue trousers. And Jake's oldest possession.

"You'll have to wait a minute," Mum shouted back. She sipped her coffee slowly. "I never knew sorting out jumble could be so exhausting."

All of a sudden Jake had that sinking feeling.
HE'D sorted out a big bag of jumble, too.
And Wilfred had been 'helping'.

What if Wilfred had got mixed up with the
UNWANTED books and toys? What if he'd
disappeared in the dustbin sack that had been
taken to the Organiser?

Jake and Mum looked through every room in
the house together. They came across all sorts
of interesting things! But they didn't find
Wilfred.

Jake was in such a panic that Mum took him to the phone box in his pyjamas.

"I'm sorry," said the Organiser. "The jumble's already been collected and locked in the church hall."

"Don't worry," Mum told Jake. "The jumble sale is tomorrow. We'll be first there."

But Mum and Jake were late. Huge roadworks held up their bus. By the time they reached the hall, it was packed.

"Let's start this end," said Mum. They dived into the crowd.

Jake found himself by a lady selling sweaters and cardigans.

"I'm looking for Wilfred," he said.

"Over there!" boomed Cardigans. She pushed Jake towards an ancient fridge.

39

"I'm looking for Wilfred," he repeated.

"That's ME!" beamed a man by the fridge.
"I'm Electrical."

"But I want my BEAR," said Jake.

"Oh, the BEAR!" said Wilfred. He pointed to
a lady with long hair.

Jake squeezed his way across.

"Tickets here!" cried Long Hair. "Buy a ticket here and win this ADORABLE teddy bear."

But the bear in the raffle was bright yellow and brand new. Jake bit his lip.

"What is it, dear?" asked another Helper.

"It's my bear," whispered Jake. "I've lost my bear."

"Speak up," cried the Helper.

41

"He's got… BLUE TROUSERS," yelled Jake above the din.

"Just a minute." The Helper swooped onto her table.

"Sorry," she announced. "All the blue ones have gone. How about this nice pink pair… with blue flowers?"

Jake took one look and fled.

"WHOOPS!" He crashed into Mum right by the books and toys table. Jake and Mum caught sight of Wilfred at exactly the same moment.

"THAT BEAR!" they cried together and reached forwards.

"Sorry," said Books and Toys. "But that bear is not for sale."

Jake's face fell. Mum drew herself up.

"You see," went on Books and Toys, "it must be a mistake. He was in my jumble bag. But he couldn't possibly be an UNWANTED bear. So I'm saving him… till his Owner turns up."

Jake and Mum both started talking at once.

Books and Toys smiled apologetically. "You do understand," she said, "that with such a SPECIAL bear, I have to be SURE."

Books and Toys bent down and whispered in Jake's ear. She'd taken a good look at Wilfred and asked Jake a question. Only Wilfred's Owner could know the answer.

Jake went pink, but whispered back. Books and Toys chuckled.

"He's your bear, all right," she said. And handed Wilfred over.

Jake didn't let Wilfred out of his sight for the rest of the day. He clutched him extra tightly at bedtime.

"I WISH I knew what you told the Books and Toys lady," said Mum.

Jake went pink again and snuggled down.

"Some things between a Bear and his Owner," he said, "are… PRIVATE!"

"Quite right too," said Mum. And kissed them both goodnight.

The owl who snored

Oliver was a fluffy new owl. And his parents were very proud of him.

But, when he was a few weeks old, Oliver developed a problem. He began to snore!

"AAAAH!" yawned Mr Owl each evening. "I hardly slept a wink."

"AAAAH!" groaned Mrs Owl. "Is that the time already?"

Oliver's parents tried everything.

Oliver slept facing the sun and then with his back to it.

His parents grew so desperate that they took it in turns… to tap Oliver on the beak and to shout: "DON'T SNORE, OLIVER!"

Then one day, when Oliver was making even more noise than usual, an old sheep leaned through the fence.

"Does anyone up there want any wool?" she bleated.

Oliver carried on snoring. But his parents woke with a start.

47

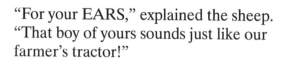

"For your EARS," explained the sheep.
"That boy of yours sounds just like our
farmer's tractor!"

Oliver's parents blushed. Then they flew down
quietly to collect some wool.

"Take some off my *number*," offered the
sheep. "My coat's thickest there."

Mr and Mrs Owl tugged gently at the wool.
By the time they had finished Oliver was just
waking up.

"Mmmmm," he stretched comfortably on the branch. "What a lovely day's sleep!"

Oliver's parents yawned all night long. They couldn't wait for bedtime.

"Oooooh, twit, twooooh! That tickles!" they giggled, as they stuffed each other's ears.

But the wool didn't work! They could still hear Oliver snoring.

The old sheep shook her head sadly.

"This case is BEYOND ME," she declared. "I'm off… out of earshot."

49

But not long afterwards the sheep had troubles of her own. She woke up the owls to tell them all about it.

"POOH!" shrieked Mr Owl.

"Dear ME!" squealed Mrs Owl.

"ATISHOO!" sneezed Oliver. "ATISHOO!"

"Dip!" said the old sheep glumly. "Our farmer's just dipped us. It's meant to make us clean and healthy."

"POOH!" cried the owls together. "Is it always that strong?"

The sheep gave a tired smile.

"I went round three times," she said.
"Because no one could read my number!"

Mr and Mrs Owl shuffled uncomfortably on
the branch. They began to feel guilty. So they
ignored the horrible smell and stayed awake
to cheer up the sheep.

They forgot all about Oliver until Mrs Owl
felt a gentle pressure against her wing.

"LOOK!" she whispered with great
excitement. "Oliver's asleep. And he's…
NOT SNORING."

The old sheep drew herself up proudly.

"It must be the dip," she announced. "I can't
recommend it for a bath. But at least it's
cleared Oliver's nose!"

Our babysitter

Our sitter doesn't say, "Not now",
Or turn the telly low.
Our sitter doesn't groan, "It's late,
So, off to bed you go!"

Our sitter doesn't make us wash,
Or shout, "Clean out the bath!"
Our sitter likes to tell us jokes,
And always makes us laugh.

Our sitter sometimes raids the fridge,
We all join in the snack.
And if it makes our baby burp,
We pat her on the back.

Our sitter rides a motorbike,
He lets us share his gum.
And when our sitter sits with us,
We NEVER miss our mum!

Animal
Stories

Contents

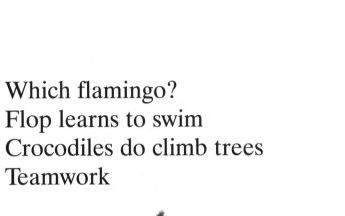

Brown Bear's visit

Brown Bear had just finished breakfast.

"That was horrible," he grumbled. "What's next?"

"Next," said Mum, "you can go to the playground while I tidy up."

Brown Bear began to grizzle. "Same old friends, same old slide. It wouldn't be so bad if we had a climbing frame."

Brown Bear was grouchy all day. Then, when he got home, Mum sent him off to the waterfall… for a shower!

Brown Bear came back damp and grumpy. He grumbled as he gobbled his supper. He grizzled as he snuggled into bed. Mum tucked him in and told him a story.

"AAAAH! That WAS boring," he yawned. And fell asleep.

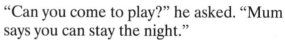

Next morning Brown Bear had a visitor. It was his cousin from across the mountain.

"Can you come to play?" he asked. "Mum says you can stay the night."

Brown Bear barely said goodbye to his mum. He didn't wave to his friends on the slide. He just jogged along beside his cousin and asked what they were going to do first.

"First," said Brown Bear's cousin, "I'll show you our climbing frame. Then I'll take you home… to meet the twins."

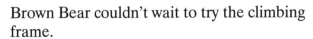

Brown Bear couldn't wait to try the climbing frame.

"It's easy," said his cousin. "Just watch me and my friends."

But Brown Bear had never turned a somersault before. He fell off and bumped his nose!

Brown Bear's cousin didn't seem to notice. He carried on clambering with his friends until it was time to go home.

Brown Bear smelt something cooking and cheered up at the thought of food. But Auntie was all behind.

"Those twins," she cried, "are ALWAYS under my feet."

But then she had a brainwave. "Why don't you big bears take the little ones to the river? You can bath them for me. And bath yourselves at the same time."

"Why can't we go to the waterfall?" cried Brown Bear. "I don't like rivers."

"Because we don't have one," said Auntie, simply. She began to tidy up.

As soon as they reached the river, the twins squirted Brown Bear and his cousin. Then, just when it was time to go home, they rolled on the bank and got all dirty again.

Brown Bear had NEVER been so cross or so hungry.

"Here we are at last," said Auntie. But, as soon as she brought in supper, the other bears swooped like vultures.

Brown Bear's tummy was still rumbling when he went to bed. It was so dark he couldn't even see his cousin.

"Can I have a story?" he called out.

But Auntie was already snoring. And so were all the other bears.

The next day Brown Bear's cousin led him along the track. He pointed in the direction of Brown Bear's home. "Look," he said. "Your mum's coming to meet you."

Brown Bear barely said goodbye to his cousin.
He bounded along the track as fast as his legs
would carry him.

"It IS good to see you, Brown Bear," said
Mum. "Now what would you like to do first?"

Brown Bear nestled up to Mum. Then he put
his nose in the air and breathed in the sweet
smells of home.

"LOVELY FRIENDS, LOVELY SLIDE,
LOVELY WATERFALL, LOVELY MEALS
AND LOVELY STORIES!" he cried.

"And I want to do it ALL first!"

Hippo hiccups

Hic, said the hippo,
I don't know what I've done.
I've only played, *hic,* in the mud
And lazed, *hic,* in the sun.

Hic, said the hippo,
However can I eat?
I'm, *hic, hic,* hiccing from my nose
Right down, *hic,* to my feet.

Hic, said the hippo,
I'll stand, *hic,* on my head.
I'll MAKE those hiccups better
Oh, *hic…* they're worse instead!

Hic, said the hippo,
I'll try a tiny drink.
Perhaps some, *hic, hic,* water
Will make my hiccups shrink.

Ssssh, said the hippo,
Is it too soon to say?
I think the worst is over
Hooray! Hip, *hic,* hooray!

The singing lion

The little lion loved singing.
But he couldn't sing
in tune!

"Shall we have a singsong?"
he asked his mum.
But Mum couldn't face it.
"Not now, dear, I'm
starting one of my
headaches."

The little lion wandered off, humming under his breath.

"Shall we have a singsong?" he asked the giraffe.

The giraffe bent her long neck to listen. But she soon shot back up again.

"Not now, thank you," she whispered. "I'm getting a sore throat."

"Help!" thought the little lion. "I hope I don't lose MY voice."

"Shall we have a singsong?" he asked the zebra. "It goes like this… "

But the zebra was already into his stride. "Not now," he called. "I must go for a run."

All the other animals suddenly disappeared, too. The little lion couldn't understand it. But then he came across an explorer and a film crew.

"Shall we have a singsong?" roared the little lion.

But the explorer and his film crew panicked. They dropped their megaphone and fled.

From then on there was pandemonium on the plain.

"SHALL WE HAVE A SINGSONG?" bellowed the little lion.

It was SUCH fun singing through the megaphone.

At last a crafty old snake decided to brave the din. She persuaded the little lion to follow her to a lonely cave.

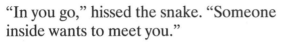

"In you go," hissed the snake. "Someone inside wants to meet you."

The little lion stepped forward nervously. "It's very dark," he whispered.

"That's because my friend is shy," replied the snake. "He doesn't like to be seen. But he does like a singsong!"

The little lion rushed inside and sang at the top of his voice. And to his joy another voice joined in. It even knew all the same songs.

The little lion spent many happy hours singing in the cave with his friend. The other animals decided not to tell him that it was really an echo of his own voice.

So once more there was peace on the plain.

71

A surprise for a tortoise

Nimble and Leaf were chatting about birthdays. Leaf had begun the conversation because it was going to be HER birthday very soon.

"This year," she said proudly, "I shall be ONE HUNDRED years old. And I want to do something special!"

"Leave things to me," said Nimble (who was a nippy ninety-three). "I'll fix you the tortoise treat of a lifetime."

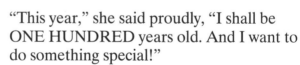

Nimble thought long and hard about Leaf's birthday. She asked the other animals for suggestions. But no one had any bright ideas.

By the night before Leaf's birthday Nimble was desperate. She tossed and turned in her shell. Then, just before midnight, she thought of the PERFECT birthday surprise.

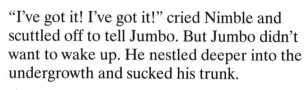

"I've got it! I've got it!" cried Nimble and scuttled off to tell Jumbo. But Jumbo didn't want to wake up. He nestled deeper into the undergrowth and sucked his trunk.

Next Nimble went to see Chimp. She found him burying bananas at the bottom of his tree. But, when Chimp heard the rustle of tiny feet, he fell flat on his back. And started snoring.

Last Nimble went looking for Parrot. Parrot was wide awake, all right. But he was gazing at his reflection in the lake. And practising his best joke.

Nimble couldn't get a word in edgeways.

"Bother!" she cried. "I shall have to catch them all in the morning."

At first light Nimble explained her plan to Jumbo.

"A SURPRISE FOR A TORTOISE!" he boomed. "I'm much too high and mighty for that."

"Fair enough," said Nimble. Then she added politely, "I do hope I didn't disturb you last night… when you were sucking your trunk."

"WAIT!" Jumbo didn't want the other animals to know he still sucked his trunk, so he agreed to help.

Next Nimble went to see Chimp.

"What a lot of fuss about nothing!" he cried. "And, anyway, I shall be busy."

"Of course," said Nimble politely. "You'll be busy… burying bananas."

"WAIT!" Chimp didn't want the other animals to know about his secret hoard, so he agreed to help.

Nimble found Parrot by the lake.

"A treat, a treat," he squawked. "I'll give YOU a treat!"

"Yes, please," said Nimble politely. "Will you tell me that joke… the one you were practising last night?"

"WAIT!" Parrot didn't want the other animals to think him vain, so he agreed to help, too.

When Leaf woke up on her birthday, everything was ready.

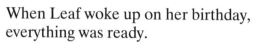

"Close your eyes," said Nimble. "Here comes your surprise."

"Is it a big surprise?" asked Leaf.

"Quite big," said Nimble. "You can open your eyes now."

As Leaf looked up, Jumbo strode forwards. On his back were Chimp and Parrot.

Leaf looked confused. "What is it?" she asked.

"It's a RIDE ON A JUMBO," said Jumbo proudly. "I'm going to take you on the trip of a lifetime."

"But, what if I fall off?" asked Leaf. "And how will I get up there?"

"That's MY job!" cried Chimp. "I'll carry you onto Jumbo's back. And then I'll be your seat belt."

"And I'M going to be your guide to all the sights!" squawked Parrot. He tapped his beak with a knowing air.

"Did you enjoy it?" asked Nimble when they all came back.

"It was a WONDERFUL birthday surprise!"
cried Leaf. Then she looked shyly at her
friend. "Do you know any whales or dolphins,
Nimble? Because next year I should like to
take a CRUISE!"

Which flamingo?

The flamingos lined up
In a long, long row.
There was something important
They needed to know.

"Oh please, Mr Toucan,
Do tell us, please.
Which of us here has
The knobbliest knees?"

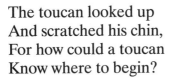

The toucan looked up
And scratched his chin,
For how could a toucan
Know where to begin?

There were so many knobbles
On so many knees.
He began to feel hot
In spite of the breeze.

The flamingos grew restless.
"This is no fun.
For heaven's sake, Toucan
Tell us who's won."

So Toucan spoke up
And prayed he would please.
"You've ALL got the best and
The knobbliest knees!"

Flop learns to swim

Flop, the penguin, was nervous. It was time for his first swimming lesson.

"Hurry up!" called Dad at the top of his voice. "We don't want to be late."

"Hey! What about breakfast?" cried Flop. "We don't want to be hungry either."

"Just a small one," said Dad. "Too much food will give you cramp."

Down by the sea Flop got cold feet. He tugged at Dad's flipper.

"The water's FFFFREEZING!" said Flop. "Let's go home for more breakfast."

Dad took no notice. "The first thing to learn about swimming," he began, "is to relax."

But Flop didn't feel relaxed. He felt cold and wobbly. "What if I can't do it, Dad?" he whispered. "Everyone will laugh."

Just then a group of young penguins rushed past him.

"Watch this, Flop," they cried.

One by one the penguins dived into the sea. And covered Flop with spray.

"BRRRR! BRRRR!" Flop's beak began to chatter.

"Please, Dad," said Flop. "I want to go home."

But Dad was beginning to enjoy himself. "Never mind THEM," he said. "Watch ME."

Flop shivered miserably on the shore.

"Splish, DEEP, splosh, BREATHS." Dad began his demonstration. "Splish, CHIN, splosh, UP," he gasped. "Now YOU try, Flop."

Flop took a deep breath and waded towards Dad. But then he tripped and fell beak first into the water.

"HELP! HELP!" yelled Flop. "I'M DROWNING."

84

Dad scooped Flop out of the water. He patted him firmly on the back.

Flop choked and spluttered.

"I don't want to do any more swimming today," he whispered.

Now it was Dad's turn to choke and splutter.

"Call THAT swimming?" he bellowed. "Now, for heaven's sake, Flop, please CONCENTRATE!"

Flop tried harder and harder to swim. Dad tried harder and harder to teach him. But the harder Dad tried, the louder he shouted.

"Please, Dad," said Flop. "I'm not DEAF. I just can't swim."

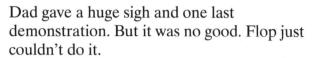

Dad gave a huge sigh and one last demonstration. But it was no good. Flop just couldn't do it.

Dad waddled back to the shore. He sat down with a plop… the picture of disappointment.

Just at that moment another father arrived in the bay. His young daughter was swimming strongly beside him.

Flop's dad groaned and put his head in his flippers.

86

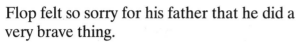

Flop felt so sorry for his father that he did a very brave thing.

He bobbed carefully out to sea until the water reached right up to his beak. Then he swam along… with one foot on the bottom.

"Look at me! Look at me!" quavered Flop.

"WELL DONE, FLOP!" beamed Dad. He started to strut along the shore.

"Well done!" beamed the other dad. Then he took a closer look at Flop's father.

"Why, it's old Shortie!" he boomed. "I haven't seen you since those TERRIBLE swimming lessons. Our fathers nearly deafened us. Don't you remember? In the end we went along with one foot on the bottom… just to keep them happy!"

"AHEM, AHEM, AHEM!" For some reason Flop's dad couldn't stop coughing.

Flop was fascinated. Fancy that penguin calling his dad "Shortie." And fancy Dad swimming along with HIS foot on the bottom.

Flop began to feel relaxed. He wriggled his toes in the water and gave a little chortle. Then, all of a sudden, he gave a great WHOOP of delight.

"I'M SWIMMING! I'M SWIMMING!" he cried.

And, as he shouted, Flop flipped onto his back and waved both feet in the air… just to prove it!

Crocodiles do climb trees

"Don't do that, Mum," said Snappy. "Crocodiles aren't meant to dance. They're meant to slither and be menacing."

But Snappy's mum didn't want to slither. She didn't feel menacing.

"Slow, slow, quick quick, slow." Snappy's mum waltzed up to a clump of trees and put a flower behind her ear.

Snappy groaned. "Leave it out, Mum. What if any of my friends see you?"

Snappy's mum didn't mind WHO saw her. She carried on dancing all afternoon. Then, instead of slithering in a nice, menacing sort of way, she shot up the nearest tree.

"Mum, Mum," shrieked Snappy. "CROCODILES DON'T CLIMB TREES!"

"This one does," said Mum. "It makes me feel good. I like the view."

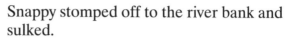

Snappy stomped off to the river bank and sulked.

"Come on in!" cried a voice from the water. "It's a lovely day for a dip."

Snappy slithered down the bank. He liked the look of this new friend.

"He's just my sort of croc," thought Snappy. And, before he knew it, Snappy had invited him over... the next afternoon.

All night long Snappy worried and wriggled. However could he make his mum behave in front of his new friend?

Snappy swung into action at the crack of dawn.

"Wake up, Mum!" he cried. "We'll dance all morning. Then you'll be too tired to dance this afternoon!"

"Slow, slow, quick quick, slow." Snappy and Mum danced themselves dizzy.

"Let's have lunch in that tree," cried Snappy at last. "Then you won't need a climb later!"

"PHEW!" Snappy got Mum back on the ground just in time.

"I think I hear someone," he said. "Now, please remember… CROCODILES DON'T CLIMB TREES!"

"THIS ONE DOES!" boomed a friendly voice.

Snappy couldn't believe his ears. It was his new friend's mum.

"Slow, slow, quick quick, slow!" She was dancing along in front of her son to show him the way.

Snappy's new friend groaned and blushed. But Snappy gave his widest grin.

"We're going swimming," he called over his shoulder.

But, of course, Snappy's mum didn't hear him. She was too busy showing HER new friend the view… from her favourite treetop!

Teamwork

Two leopards were wearing
A terrible frown.
They wriggled and jiggled
And jumped up and down.

They twisted, INSISTED,
"I CAN count my spots,"
Then tumbled and grumbled,
"I'm tied up in knots."

They growled and they scowled,
They hadn't a clue.
Then all of a sudden,
They knew what to do.

They bounced and announced
And shook their great paws,
"You can count *my* spots…
And I will count yours!"

Farmyard
Stories

Contents

Philippa's ride

"OUCH!" squealed Philippa Piglet. "I've cut my trotter."

"Never mind," said Mum briskly. She began to lick it better.

But, when Farmer Fred saw the cut, he was worried. So he drove Philippa to the vet.

At bedtime Philippa's brothers admired the bandage. But Philippa simply stared into the distance. "It was WONDERFUL!" she sighed.

"What was?" chorused her brothers.

"My ride in Farmer Fred's landrover," whispered Philippa and promptly fell asleep.

From then on all Philippa could think about was travel.

But Philippa's trotter had healed now. There was no need to visit the vet again. So, whenever Farmer Fred found her by the landrover, he always said the same thing. "Come on, let's put you back where you belong."

And with that he would tuck Philippa under his arm and carry her back to her family.

"Never mind," said Mum briskly, when it happened again. She pushed an apple towards Philippa.

But Philippa DID mind and she was busy making a plan.

Early next morning the little piglet squeezed through the gate that led to the lane. Just along the lane was a bus stop. Philippa had been watching it from the farmyard.

"If I wait here long enough," she told herself, "I can have another ride!"

"Whatever next!" cried a man weighed down with parcels. He had staggered off the bus and had almost fallen over Philippa.

The bus driver jumped off, too.

"Come on," he said to Philippa. "Let's put you back where you belong." The bus driver took Philippa back to the farmyard.

"Never mind," said Mum briskly. "I've saved you an acorn."

But Philippa DID mind, because more than anything else, she still wanted to travel.

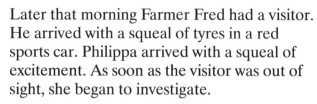

Later that morning Farmer Fred had a visitor. He arrived with a squeal of tyres in a red sports car. Philippa arrived with a squeal of excitement. As soon as the visitor was out of sight, she began to investigate.

"TOOOOOOOT!"

"Who's sounding my horn?" boomed a voice from the farmhouse door.

The visitor strode across the yard. But Philippa had already disappeared into the nearest barn where Farmer Fred's son was polishing his motorbike.

"Hello!" he chuckled. "Would you like a spin… back to where you belong?"

Philippa rushed forward eagerly. But then she froze in her tracks because Mum was standing in the doorway… looking stern!

"PHILIPPA!" she cried. "Big motorbikes are too fast and too noisy for small piglets!"

Philippa sulked all evening. She slept badly all night and woke late and grumpy next morning.

"DING-A-LING-LING! ANYONE COMING FOR A RIDE?"

It was Farmer Fred's daughter on her new bike. And behind the bike was a little trailer.

Mum nudged Philippa forward. "Go on," she said briskly.

"HOORAY!" cried Farmer Fred's daughter. She lifted Philippa up. "All the other animals ran away. But you look as if you BELONG in my trailer."

Round and round the farmyard rode the little girl and the little piglet.

They both squealed as loudly as each other. And, however hard you looked, it was quite impossible to tell which of them enjoyed it most!

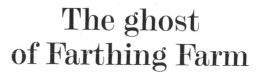

The ghost
of Farthing Farm

"Isn't it DARK?" whispered Joel. He was staying with Mike at Farthing Farm. Joel came from the town.

"Isn't it QUIET?" he whispered a few minutes later. Joel was used to street lights and traffic.

At last Mike and Joel settled down. But not for long.

"Whatever's THAT?" cried Joel. He sat up in bed and shivered. "It sounds like a ghost," he whispered, "a very unhappy ghost!"

Mike rubbed his eyes and groaned. "It's just one of the sheep bleating," he explained patiently.

Joel settled down again. But in no time at all he was digging Mike in the ribs.

"Whatever's THAT?" he cried. "It sounds like a ghost… a ghost with dreadful tummy-ache!"

"It's just one of the cows mooing," explained Mike, a little less patiently.

Joel crept out of bed and peered through the window. He thought he could see some sheep and cow shapes. Joel began to feel better.

But suddenly Mike was clutching at JOEL'S pyjamas. "Whatever's THAT?" he shrieked.

Joel smiled sleepily. "It must be one of your animals," he said.

"But it's NOT!" cried Mike. "I know all the animal noises and I've NEVER heard anything like that."

Both boys peered out gingerly. The moon came out from behind a cloud.

"HELP!" cried Mike and Joel together.

In the field opposite was a ghostly figure. It had a huge pale head, which swayed and MOANED in the moonlight.

113

All of a sudden Mum appeared outside in her dressing gown. She seemed to wrestle with the figure. And then Mike burst out laughing.

"It's Ned, our donkey!" he cried.

When Mum came back inside, she was carrying an empty potato sack.

"No wonder poor Ned was making such a strange noise," she said. "He'd been looking for scraps and got his head stuck."

Mum tucked in the boys again and smiled.

"Whoever said it's always quiet in the country?" she asked.

"Not me!" whispered Joel and fell fast asleep until morning.

Chickens

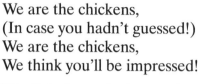

We are the chickens,
(In case you hadn't guessed!)
We are the chickens,
We think you'll be impressed!

We slide down the haystack,
We balance on the coop,
We fly in strict formation
And ALWAYS loop the loop!

We dive from the dovecot,
We stagger to a stop,
We like to chase the sheep
And then to ride on top!

We bounce on the tractor,
We give the horn a BEEP,
We gallop round the yard
And NEVER go to sleep!

We are the chickens!
Our farmer needs a rest,
But still he tells his friends,
"MY CHICKENS ARE THE BEST!"

116

Gus goes to playgroup

"I don't want to go to playgroup," said Jenny, "…not unless Gus comes."

Jenny lived on a farm and Gus was a new goat.

"Jenny," sighed Dad, "I've already explained. Playgroup is for children, not for animals."

"But it's my first day," complained Jenny. "I won't know anybody."

Dad rang up Mrs Wright, the playgroup leader, for advice.

Playgroup had already started. You could tell by the din. But Mrs Wright shouted cheerfully down the line, "That will be fine. You'd be surprised what some children bring… particularly on their first day!"

Dad, Jenny and Gus all set off for playgroup. When they arrived, Mrs Wright was ticking names on a list.

"Trevor," she smiled, "THAT'S a nice train. Paul," she went on, "I DO like your panda. And YOU must be Jenny," beamed Mrs Wright.

Then she saw Gus.

"Good heavens!" cried Mrs Wright, turning to Dad. "I thought you said Jenny was bringing a BOAT. But now I see, it's a GOAT!"

Dad began to apologise, but Mrs Wright shooed him away. "Gus can stay for today," she said.

As soon as Dad left, Gus began to explore. One of the new children began to cry. And in no time at all, half the playgroup was crying.

Suddenly the tears turned to laughter. "WHEEEE!" Gus had squeezed himself into the playgroup pushchair and was whizzing across the floor.

"Thank goodness!" cried Mrs Wright. She settled the children to play.

Jenny began a painting. But Gus wanted to help. Jenny's picture didn't turn out as she planned.

Halfway through the morning the children had a snack.

"My word!" cried Mrs Wright. "I've NEVER seen such MESSY eaters!"

Suddenly Gus swept along like a hoover. Crumbs, crisps, apple cores, banana skins… it was all the same to Gus.

"Well done, Gus!" cried Mrs Wright. She began organising the children again.

Jenny wanted to try the slide. But so did Gus.

"HELP!" cried Jenny. "We're stuck!"

Mrs Wright untangled Jenny and Gus. But another tangle had started… by the clay. Paul and Susie were fighting.

"WHEEEE, PLOP!" Susie threw Paul's panda right on top of the cupboard.

"Oh no!" cried Mrs Wright. She HATED ladders.

But, before she could fetch one, Gus leaped to the rescue. He wanted to practise his climbing and SOARED from the top of the slide… right onto the cupboard. Then he bounced back down again. And panda bounced down, too!

"What a relief," said Mrs Wright. She looked at her watch and lined up the chairs for storytime.

Jenny wanted to sit next to Susie. But Gus pushed in first, just as Dad arrived.

"I do hope Gus hasn't been a nuisance," he began.

Mrs Wright shook her head and beamed. But, before she could say anything, Jenny piped up, "Yes, he has, Dad. And tomorrow I want to paint and go down the slide and make new friends ON MY OWN!"

So Gus didn't go to playgroup again. But, later that year, Jenny invited her new friends to the farm.

The playgroup children loved meeting the animals. But most of all they enjoyed seeing Gus again.

"Hasn't he grown!" they cried.

"Yes, he has," said Mrs Wright. She watched Gus charge round the farmyard. "And, although Gus is a WONDERFUL goat, he is definitely… TOO BIG FOR PLAYGROUP!"

The sheep who liked to be different

Scruff liked to be different. If the rest of the flock sat down for a chat and a chew, then Scruff went for a jog. If the other sheep started a stampede, Scruff simply turned her back and munched quietly in a corner.

She gave the sheepdog a terrible time. Whenever he got the sheep running one way, Scruff changed direction and sent them all scattering.

"I've never known a sheep with such a mind of her own!" said Farmer Field.

One warm, sunny day an interesting piece of news reached the flock. It was time for their first shearing. And the shearer was coming the next day.

This news set the sheep bleating. Some of them didn't want to be shorn.

"We'll look DAAAAAAFT!" they complained.

Others were all for it. "This weather is too hot!" they cried. "We want to feel cool!"

But on one thing the sheep were generally agreed. If Farmer Field had decided to shear them, then shorn they would be.

Scruff, of course, had other ideas. She was proud of her thick, curly coat and had no intention of losing it.

Early next morning Scruff set off… to find a hiding place. After a time she came to an old toolshed. The door was half-open. So, with a quick glance over her shoulder, she nipped inside.

"Perfect!" she announced and settled down under the workbench for a snooze.

By lunchtime the shearer was well on with his work. Farmer Field had his hands full helping and in the excitement NO ONE missed Scruff.

It was another blazing hot day. Very soon cheerful cries of "THAAAT'S MUUUUCH BEEEEETTER!" could be heard all over the fields.

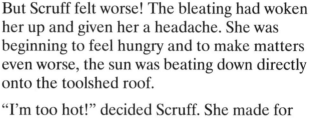

But Scruff felt worse! The bleating had woken her up and given her a headache. She was beginning to feel hungry and to make matters even worse, the sun was beating down directly onto the toolshed roof.

"I'm too hot!" decided Scruff. She made for the toolshed door. But a rare gust of wind had blown it shut. Scruff was a prisoner!

She clambered onto the workbench and looked miserably through the window. In the distance she could see all her friends.

"If only I could be shorn!" sighed Scruff.

"Rattle, rattle, click!" Scruff jumped down eagerly from the bench. Someone was at the shed door.

It was Mrs Field, the farmer's wife. She didn't see Scruff for dust.

"ZOOOOM!" Scruff shot out of the shed and POUNDED across the field.

The shearer was just packing up his equipment.

"I might have guessed!" said Farmer Field.

The sheepdog sniffed in disgust.

"I'm sorry," said the shearer. "My blade's blunt. And it's my last one. I don't see HOW I can make this sheep look like the rest."

Farmer Field turned to the shearer and grinned.

"Now, don't you worry about THAT," he said. "Scruff LIKES to be different."

So, in the end, Scruff had the best of both worlds. She was soon cool and comfortable again. But, because the shearer's blade was blunt, Scruff was given a style… ALL OF HER OWN!

The chewalong song

CHEW, CHEW,
I DO love a CHEW!
There's nothing like breakfast
All covered in dew.
There's no need to buy it,
Or even to fry it,
So why don't you try it
And CHEW!

MUNCH, MUNCH,
I DO love a MUNCH!
There's nothing like clover
For flavouring lunch.
Although it grows thickly
You won't find it sickly,
So gather some quickly
And MUNCH!

GRAZE, GRAZE,
I DO love a GRAZE!
There's nothing quite like it
On warm, sunny days.
So please share my dinner,
This field is a winner!
We'll never grow thinner,
Let's GRAZE!

135

Too busy to hiss

"Ready!" cried Mother Goose. The goslings stood tall.

"Steady!" she yelled. The goslings leaned forwards.

"GO!" thundered Mum. And the goslings all HISSED… all except Henry.

"Sorry, Mum," said Henry. "I'm too busy to hiss. I'm meeting my friend the lamb. She's teaching me to jump."

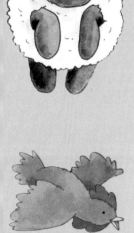

"HENRY!" called Mum after him. "Just be on time for your NEXT lesson."

But Henry was LATE for his next lesson. And, when he got there, he couldn't concentrate.

"HISSSSSS!" went Henry's brothers.

"One, two, three, four, five, seven, ten," mumbled Henry. He watched the ducklings carefully as they waddled past.

"HENRY!" cried Mum. "What DO you think you're doing?"

"Sorry, Mum," said Henry. "I'm too busy to hiss. I'm learning to count."

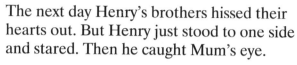
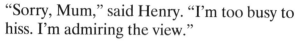

The next day Henry's brothers hissed their hearts out. But Henry just stood to one side and stared. Then he caught Mum's eye.

"Sorry, Mum," said Henry. "I'm too busy to hiss. I'm admiring the view."

"HENRY!" bellowed Mum. "Go and admire the view somewhere else. I am VERY cross."

Henry didn't like the look in Mum's eye. He scuttled off so fast that he bumped bang into some bales of straw.

Henry picked himself up. But something was wrong. He could just see a thin curl of smoke. It was coming from the straw!

"HELP!" thought Henry. "It's a fire!"

Henry didn't hesitate. He jumped high into the air and gave the loudest HISSSSSSSSSS ever!

138

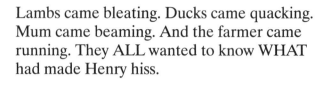

Lambs came bleating. Ducks came quacking. Mum came beaming. And the farmer came running. They ALL wanted to know WHAT had made Henry hiss.

As soon as he saw the smoke, the farmer fetched his fire extinguisher.

"SWOOSH, SWOOSH, SWOOOOOOSH!" He squirted the bales and the danger was over.

"Ready!" cried Mum at bedtime.

"Steady!" cried the goslings.

"HENRY is a HERO!" they all cheered.

But Henry didn't feel like a hero. He just felt happy… and TIRED!